EMMA SWINGS

Written and illustrated by LOU ALPERT

Whispering Coyote Press Inc./New York

Published by Whispering Coyote Press Inc.
P.O. Box 2159, Halesite, New York 11743-2159
Text copyright © 1991 by Lou Alpert
Illustrations copyright © 1991 by Lou Alpert
Printed in the United States of America
ISBN 1-879085-04-6

A portion of the proceeds from this book will go to
Girls Adventure Trails in Dallas, Texas.

To Linda Sue Lyne

I start to swing without a sound,

My feet go up, my feet go down.

My head goes back, my legs go out,

As I begin to sing and shout!

"Hello!" to the birds. "Hello!" to the trees.

"You're higher than me, but wait and see!"

I swing thru the air, I stretch my toes.

They touch the treetops.

But still I go and go and go,

Swinging high, swinging low,

To and fro, to and fro,

Swinging higher than anyone knows.

Soon I'm swinging above the trees.

The air is warm, I feel a breeze.

A bird flies by singing of song,

And I keep swinging short and long.

Looking down I see the land —

Mountains, trees, oceans, and sand.

I watch a boat head out to sea,

Headed for spots unknown to me.

I see my brothers leaving school,

And a great big truck delivering fuel.

Now I'm flying thru the sky,

The clouds begin to puff me high.

They puff and blow, and puff and blow,

But still I go and go and go,

Swinging high, swinging low,

To and fro, to and fro.

Soon I see the clouds below,

Smiling up to me in rows,

They see me pass and wave good-bye.

Further down a jet zooms by.

Stars surround me, sleeping away.

Their work begins at the end of the day.

Peaceful little faces glow.

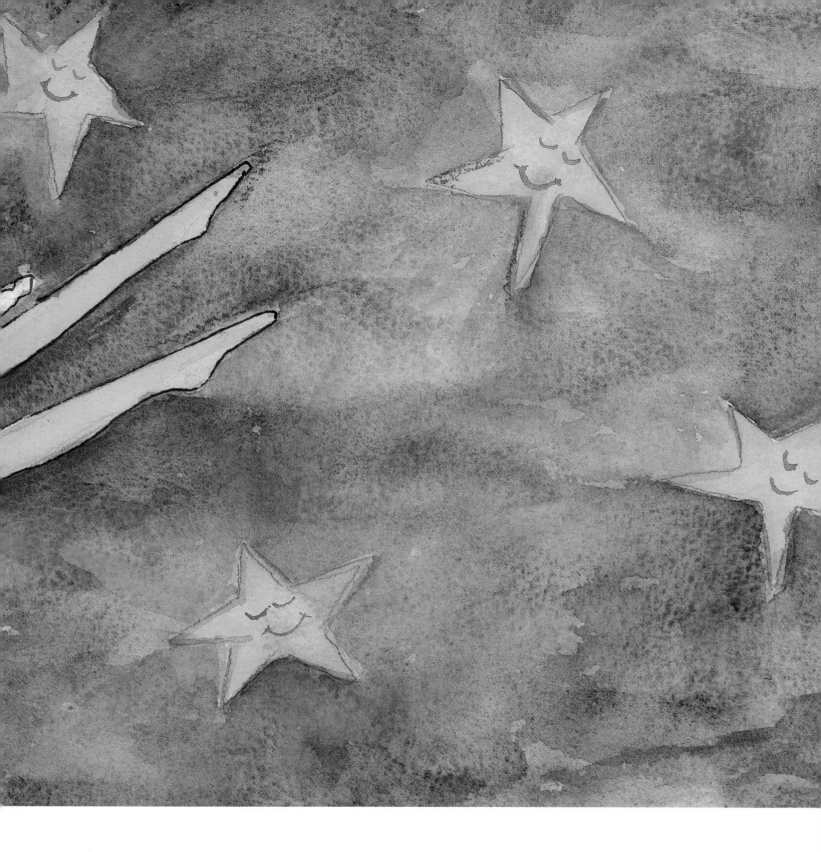

But still I go, and go, and go,

Swinging high, swinging low,

To and fro, to and fro.

My head thrown back, I close my eyes.

I feel my body sink and rise.

A voice rings out from down below,

A loving voice — one I know.

The voice begins to pull me down,

Closer and closer to the ground,

Now I go, and go, and go,

Swinging high, swinging low,

Down I go, down I go,

Towards the earth and trees below.

Now my name is loud and clear,

"Emma come home, it's late my dear."

I open my eyes, my mother is there,

Arms reaching out as I fly thru the air.

Bump! My feet are on the ground,

I open my eyes and I look around.

Up above I see the trees,

    Their leaves smile down as they sway in the breeze.

I run to my mother as our eyes meet,

She gives me a hug and we cross the street.

Safely home she holds me tight.

We gaze at the stars and say, "good night!"